BRANDY AND HER SUPER HERO

Written by Nathan and
Keven McTaggart

Illustrated by Aspenwood
Elementary School
2018/19 Division 2

Brandy and Her Super Hero
Copyright © 2019 by Nathan's Super Heroes Book Series
www.NathansSuperHeroes.com

ISBN
978-0-2288-1325-5 (Paperback)
978-0-2288-1326-2 (eBook)

Other Books by
Nathan and Keven McTaggart

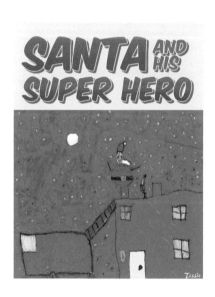

Net proceeds to the
BC Burn Fund

Net proceeds to the
Canucks for Kids Fund

Net proceeds of the sale of this book will be donated to the
Pacific Assistance Dogs Society
And
Firefighters Without Borders Canada

This book is dedicated to all the people and their fur families who are affected by natural disaster. We would also like to give a huge shout out to the dedicated first responders who risk their lives to keep us safe.

Dear Brandy,

You had quite the summer in Williams Lake. Your agility training really came in handy.

What I particularly like is how the community of first responders come together when there is an emergency. This book is based around a forest fire. But they are also there for other natural and not so natural disasters such as hurricane, tsunamis and earthquakes.

Nathan

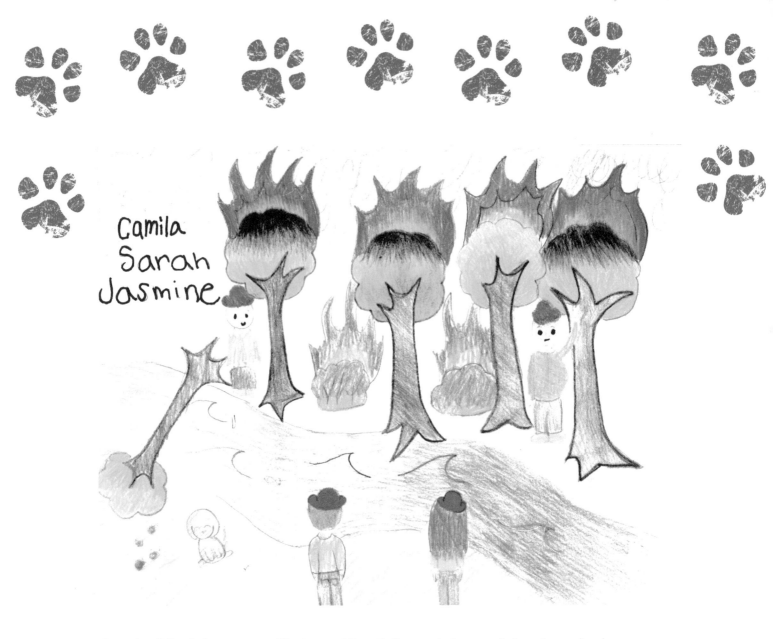

Camila
Sarah
Jasmine

Smoke filled the air as Chris and Ivy followed the path back to the basecamp after a long, hot day of work. Chris and Ivy were firefighters from Ontario who had come to the Williams Lake, British Columbia area to help with the summer's forest fires.

As they were walking, they heard faint cries for help echoing through the canyon. "Help, elp, elp, elp. Over here, ere, ere, ere." As they rushed towards the cries for help, they saw two fellow firefighters trapped on the other side of the river. There was no escape for them. In front of them was a river that was running too swiftly for them to cross. Behind them was the forest fire, burning out of control.

Alan

"Nathan, Ben, what happened?" called out Chris.

"We were out on patrol putting out spot fires well behind the main fire when suddenly, the winds shifted and pushed the fire straight towards us. Now we are trapped," Nathan replied.

"I have a rescue line," Ivy called out. "I will throw it to you." After Nathan tied one end of the rescue line to a nearby tree, Ivy hurled the rest of the line with all her might but could only get it about half way across. It was just too heavy.

"I have an idea," said Nathan. "Let's tie one end of this lighter line to a stick and the other end to the rescue line. Then we can throw the lighter line to you and you can pull the rescue line across." After one attempt they realized that the lighter line would never reach the other side. It was just too short.

As the four firefighters were trying to figure out the best way to get Nathan and Ben to safety, a dog appeared from out of the woods. She was a rather large dog and gold in colour. She had been watching the firefighters trying to play catch and thought that it would only be fair to give the two on the other side of the river a turn. So, she picked up the stick in her teeth and carefully crossed a very thin, half burned tree that had fallen across the river and dropped the stick in front of Ben. Then she carefully returned to the other side of the river and sat at Ivy's feet.

After Ben securely tied the rescue line to a tree on his side of the river, Nathan and Ben attached their safety harnesses to the line and, one at a time, crossed the river to safety.

While Nathan, Ben and Chris gathered up their equipment, Ivy stayed with the dog. She wanted to make sure that the dog went back to the base camp with them so that she could be safe from the wild fires.

"Good dog," said Ivy, as she petted her new friend. Ivy felt a collar and dog tags under the dog's thick fur. "Brandy," said Ivy as she read the tag. "Thank you Brandy. Without your help, my friends would still be trapped on the other side of that river."

Soon the four firefighters and Brandy were back on the path heading towards the basecamp. They were almost back when Brandy stopped in her tracks and looked into the woods. "What's up girl?" Chris inquired. Brandy glanced back at the group, and then she darted into the woods. The firefighters chased after her, being careful not to lose sight of her in the thick smoke. As quickly as she had taken off, she stopped and stared at a bush.

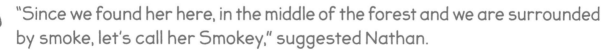

"What is it Brandy?" asked Nathan. Brandy glanced back at them and then she stared even more intensely into the bush. Curious to see what had caught Brandy's attention, Ben spread the branches and found a small black and white dog hiding under the bush. Ben bent down and carefully picked up the frightened old dog. "Does she have a dog tag?" inquired Nathan.

"No," said Ben. "I wonder what we should call her."

"Since we found her here, in the middle of the forest and we are surrounded by smoke, let's call her Smokey," suggested Nathan.

"How did Brandy know she was here?" asked Ivy.

"Did you know that a dog can hear four times the distance that a human can?" answered Chris. "And they can hear higher pitched sounds that we can't too. I guess Brandy could hear Smokey when all we could hear was our talking and footsteps."

Before long, the four firefighters and the two dogs were back at basecamp. Chris and Ivy took Smokey to get checked out while Nathan and Ben took Brandy around to introduce her to some of their friends.

Their first stop was at the tent of Joey and Sheila. Joey and Sheila were a brother and sister team of firefighters from the Metropolitan Fire Brigade in Melbourne Australia. "G'day Mate," said Joey "What's with the bitzer?"

"Bitzer?" asked Ben.

"Sorry mate, I mean dog," said Joey. "That's what we call dogs down under."

"Down under," said Nathan. "I know that one. You mean in Australia. This is Brandy. We found her down by the river," continued Nathan. "Or should I say, she found us. We think she got separated from her family during the fires."

"She has dog tags so she ain't no dingo," added in a garbled Australian accent. They all laughed at Ben's attempt to speak like an Aussie. You see, a dingo is a wild dog in Australia.

Anabella dc

Elena

"Buenas tardes, Señor Nathan!"

Nathan turned around. "Good afternoon Mister Hector!" Nathan had been on the crew who was lucky enough to drive one of their older trucks and equipment to Playa del Carmen, Mexico to donate it to the firefighters there. Firefighters in Mexico are called bomberos. Hector was one of the bomberos that Nathan had met on his trip and they had remained friends ever since. The two firefighters were very pleased to be working together again up in Nathan's home province of British Columbia.

"Tengo mucha hambre," said Hector.

"I'm very hungry too" replied Nathan.

"I hope the cook will put another shrimp on the barbie," added Sheila as they all headed over to the dining hall.

Ella, Amber, Nathalie

As they entered the dining hall, they were greeted by an older gentleman. "Hola Hector. G'day Joey and Sheila. Hello Nathan and Ben."

"Hello Uncle Gordy," they all responded. They didn't call him Uncle Gordy because he was their uncle. They called him Uncle Gordy out of respect. Uncle Gordy was not only the cook at the basecamp, he was also an old retired fire captain who had travelled the world helping out with many natural (and not so natural) disasters for many years.

"And this must be Brandy," commented Uncle Gordy.

"How did you know?" asked Ben. "Well, not only is he the talk of the camp," Uncle Gordy began, "but her owners have been here looking for her." Just then, two relieved-looking people entered the dining hall. Brandy promptly sprang to her feet and bolted across the floor to her owners.

"This is Glen and Trish, Brandy's family," said Uncle Gordy. "These two worried owners were here on vacation when they got separated from their pet, Brandy."

"Thank you for finding her," said Trish. "You guys are our heroes."

"The true hero is Brandy. If she didn't find us, we would not have made it across the river," said Ben.

"And if it wasn't for Brandy, Smokey would still be lost in the forest, lonely and afraid." Nathan added. "She might be your dog but she will always be our Super Hero."

ABOUT THE BOOK

Nathan has always regarded first responders as his Super Heroes. When we first went to visit our publisher, Tellwell Talent in Victoria BC, this was quite evident to them. They recommended that we do a full series of books about first responders.

The next summer, British Columbia was hit hard by forest fires. Nathan asked if we could write our next book about the brave men and women from around the world who come together to keep our communities safe when there is a natural disaster such as a forest fire.

Later that summer, we went to the President's Choice SuperDogs show at the PNE where Nathan was inspired to incorporate an agility trained dog into the story.

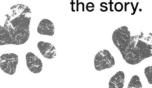

ABOUT THE AUTHORS

This is the third book by Nathan and his father, Keven, McTaggart. Nathan an energetic seventh grader who loves playing sports. When not playing hockey or lacrosse, he is eager to spend time with his family.

In Brandy and Her Super Hero, we have a number of the characters who are named after friends and relatives. Brandy was Nathan's Uncle Glen and Aunt Trish's Goldendoodle. Smokey was his grandmother's dog. Christopher is Keven's nephew and Ivy is Christopher's eight month old daughter. Ben is a very good family friend. He is also the dad of Lochlan and Giada from Nathan's and Keven's first book, Santa and His Super Hero. And lastly our cook, Uncle Gordy, was his Great Uncle Gord who was a cook for many years.

And of course, none of this would be possible without the endless support of Nathan's mother, Lucie.

ABOUT THE PACIFIC ASSISTANCE DOGS SOCIETY

Pacific Assistance Dogs Society (PADS) breeds, raises and trains fully certified assistance dogs. These amazing canine "superheroes" help their partners in all sorts of ways.

PADS service and hearing dogs provide life-changing independence to those with physical disabilities other than blindness.

PADS PTSD dogs support veterans and first responders and their accredited facility dogs work with community professionals, such as teachers, RCMP and psychologists to help support healthy communities. PADS has working teams across Canada and is a fully accredited (and active) member of Assistance Dogs International.

ABOUT FIREFIGHTERS WITHOUT BORDERS CANADA

Firefighters Without Borders Canada (FWB Canada) is a group of volunteers comprised of firefighters, emergency responders and others from across Canada and the USA. We are a registered non-profit charity based in Vancouver, British Columbia, Canada. We offer training and donated equipment to emergency service organizations in countries with a demonstrated need.

We began as Engines for El Salvador in 2003, then became Firefighters Without Borders BC in 2008 and finally in 2009 we adopted and registered our current name.

To date, we have donated over 900 tons of equipment and more than 60 emergency vehicles to 17 countries. We have also embarked on 19 overseas training missions to 6 countries.

We receive no government funding and all of our members donate their own time and money to participate in our training missions.

ABOUT THE ILLUSTRATORS

Aspenwood Elementary School's Division 2 loves draw and read, so when Nathan approached them to be the illustrators for this story, they were eager to oblige. They are so pleased to be part of Nathan's mission to give back to the first responders who give so much to our communities.

OUR SUPER HEROES
WE THANK YOU

PADS

Take your book to your local firehalls and have your Super Heroes sign it.

....

....

....

....

....

....

....

....

....

....

....

OUR SUPER HEROES

PADS

....

....

....

....

....

....

....

....

....

....

....

WE THANK YOU

PADS

....

....

....

....

....

....

....

....

....

....

....

OUR SUPER HEROES

PADS

....
....
....
....
....
....
....
....
....
....
....

WE THANK YOU

PADS

....

....

....

....

....

....

....

....

....

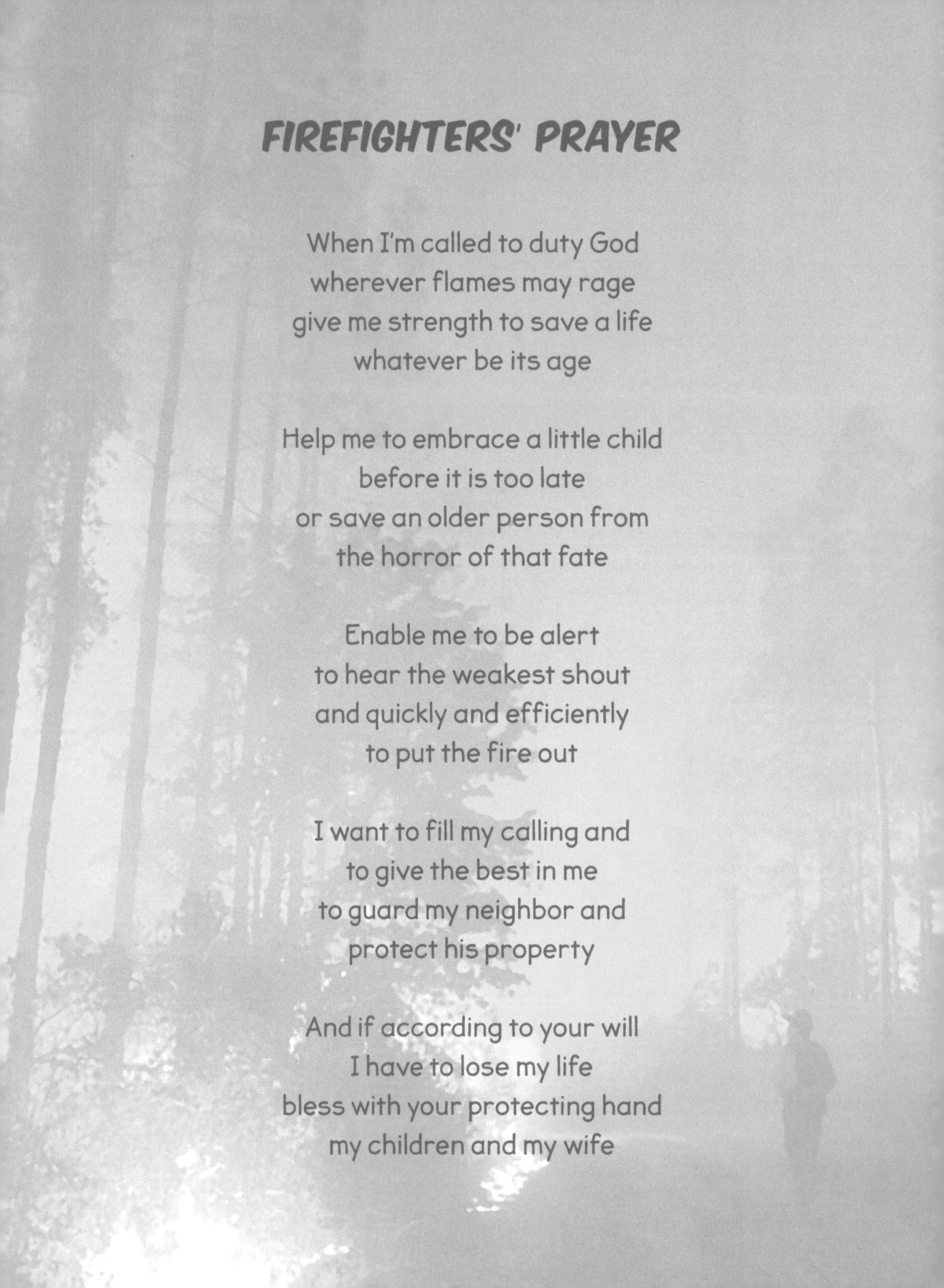

FIREFIGHTERS' PRAYER

When I'm called to duty God
wherever flames may rage
give me strength to save a life
whatever be its age

Help me to embrace a little child
before it is too late
or save an older person from
the horror of that fate

Enable me to be alert
to hear the weakest shout
and quickly and efficiently
to put the fire out

I want to fill my calling and
to give the best in me
to guard my neighbor and
protect his property

And if according to your will
I have to lose my life
bless with your protecting hand
my children and my wife

This book would not have been possible without the generosity of our backers.

Net proceeds of the sale of this book will be donated to the Pacific Assistance Dogs Society and Firefighters Without Borders Canada.

CPSIA information can be obtained
at www.ICGtesting.com
Printed in the USA
LVHW010343010519
616163LV00001B/2/P